Reach for the Stars

By Kevin Fleming

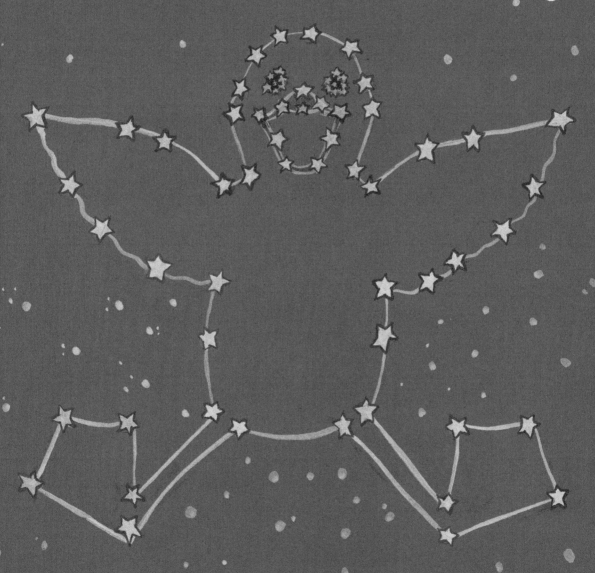

First Published by AuthorMike Ink, TBA
www.AuthorMikeInk.com

AuthorMike Ink and its logos are trademarked
by AuthorMike Ink.

Printed in the United States of America

For Connor, Mackenzie & Ryan, my wife Christina, and my parents,
with all the love that I have.

Dear Eleanor, Clara & Sam,
Capture the stars!
— Kevin J. ____

The world is so big
And you are so small

Where could you possibly
fit into it all?

"**R**each for the stars"
The people all say.

But why even try to?
They're so far away!

But maybe you're able to
reach all your dreams
Your body can do
so much more than it seems!

Think of how much
you've already done
by being a friend,
or daughter or son.

You've probably climbed to
the top of tall trees
Or used a blue marker to
draw on your knees

Or rode in a boat and
sailed the seas
Or maybe you even ate
all of your peas!

You might have swum in a pool
Or done well in school

Or used a new tool
Or one day you might even have followed a rule.

You may have rescued a bug
Or played in the mud

Or ridden trains that go "chug "
Or made someone happy with a comforting hug.

You've learned how to stand
Imagined your own land

Built castles in the sand
And you've brightened a day by holding a hand.

You've seen the earth from above
Or caught a ball with your glove

And you've done one of life's miracles:
You've given others your love.

These are quite powerful things that you've done!

Your accomplishments shine as bright as the sun.

I hope that you're proud of
all that you do

The rest of the world is
so proud of you!

Rarely you'll find those
who don't see that you're great.
They'll want you to feel bad
but don't take the bait!

While they tease you and doubt you
and tell you you're bad
Please know in your heart
the impact you've had!

Dig down inside
and find your reserve
Gain strength in the love
you so richly deserve.

Remember the compliments and praise
that you've gotten
And focus on good things
forget all the rotten.

It's easy to focus
on bad things you feel
They grow and they fester
the good things concealed.

So when someone tries
to put out your star
You have to choose
to like who you are!

You make the world such
a happier place
Just with the smile
that lights up your face

And since all that it takes
is your wonderful smile
Being yourself is
completely worthwhile!

You see all of your actions
No matter how big or small

Can make quite a difference
In the lives of us all.

You might think they don't matter
As it sometimes might seem

But all your accomplishments
Do not go unseen.

The most important thing in life is to just be yourself
More important than fame, power and wealth

Because when you are you, great things start to go
For they come from the knowledge that only you know.

There's so much that you've done,
So much more you will do

The world is much better
For the gift that is you.

So never forget how special you are
And you'll do the impossible:

You'll capture the stars.

Kevin Fleming

About the Author

If you are looking for an example of a blissful existence amidst a frenetic environment, look no further than the author, Kevin Fleming. The proud father of three incredible children, husband to an amazing wife, and owner of a loving puppy, Kevin lives in a world where giggles, shrieks, barks, laughter, and vigorous play are all in the course of a day. Because a five year-old and twin three year-olds are not exhausting enough, Kevin works full time, hopes to complete his doctorate in higher education administration in the next year, and writes children's books that he hopes will inspire laughter and happiness in readers of all ages.

Reach for the Stars is the culmination of many years of work that began on a whim while he was on a service trip in high school. His occasional tinkering with the story over the years has blossomed into a passion for writing children's books, and he hopes this will be the first of many of his books on the shelves. Reach for the Stars is the achievement of a dream, and he hopes it will encourage others to continue reaching for their own stars.

Kevin lives in Longmeadow, MA, and is a proud alumnus of James Madison University, Bowling Green State University, and a hopeful future alumnus of the University of Massachusetts Amherst.

Find out more about the author at AuthorKevinFleming.com, and follow him on Twitter @authorkfleming

Christa Whitten

To Jim,
"There he goes, turning my whole world around..."
Thank you.

About the Illustrator

Christa Whitten is an artist and illustrator living in northern Connecticut. Growing up, her parents encouraged her to pursue what makes her happy. Christa loves painting with vivid colors, meeting new people and traveling to unique places. Her favorite places are often outdoors where she can meet new feathered... and furry and slimy and scaly and flying... friends. Christa hopes this book will inspire others to reach for what makes them happy too!